STILL MORE
TALES FOR THE
MIDNIGHT HOUR

Other Scholastic paperbacks
by J. B. Stamper:

Tales for the Midnight Hour
More Tales for the Midnight Hour

STILL MORE TALES FOR THE MIDNIGHT HOUR

J.B. STAMPER

AN
APPLE
PAPERBACK

SCHOLASTIC INC.
New York Toronto London Auckland Sydney

Tailypo and *Wait Till Max Comes* are
retellings of classic American folk stories.

ISBN 0-590-42027-5

12 11 10 9 8 7 6 5 4 3 2 1   9/8 0 1 2 3 4/9

Printed in the U.S.A.   01

First Scholastic printing, October 1989

Contents

Cemetery Road

Susan looked up at the sign on the corner of her new street: Cemetery Road. At the end of the block she could see the cemetery — row after row of tombstones behind a high iron gate. Susan knew the view well by now. It was the same view she had from her bedroom window.

Just a month ago, she'd lived in a pretty house with a view of a park. Then her father had been transferred to this city. And the only house they could afford was on Cemetery Road. Susan's friends had laughed when she gave them her new address. They thought she was joking.

"Hey, aren't you the new girl?" a voice called out from behind her.

Susan turned around to see two boys and one girl riding on bicycles. She recognized them from school. They were in some of the same classes with her.

Susan nodded her head in answer to their question and kept walking.

"What's it like living on Cemetery Road?" one of the boys asked. "Pretty spooky?"

Susan felt a flush creep into her cheeks. "Not at all," she said. "I'm not one bit afraid of living here."

The girl and the boys kept riding their bikes beside Susan as she walked quickly toward her house.

"I guess you haven't heard the stories about that cemetery," the girl said. "It's haunted by a black cat."

"Sure," Susan said. "Do you expect me to believe that?"

"It's true," the other boy said. "There's a big tomb in the middle of the graveyard — it has a statue of a black cat on top of it."

"What's so scary about that?" Susan asked.

"The cat comes alive at night," the girl said. "And haunts the cemetery."

"I don't believe in things like ghosts," Susan said.

"I dare you to visit the black cat at night," one of the boys said.

Susan glared at them. "I wouldn't be afraid to do that."

"Dare you to take off its collar," the girl said. "It has a leather collar around its neck, just like a real cat."

"Bring that collar to school tomorrow," the other boy said, "and you'll prove how brave you are."

"Dare you," the girl taunted.

"It's a dare," Susan said.

She ran away from their mocking faces toward her house. She would show them that she wasn't afraid. But the thought of going into the graveyard at night made her shudder. She had to get the collar this afternoon, before it got too dark out.

Susan's house was the second from the end of the road that led into the cemetery. A rickety old house that no one lived in sat right next to the graveyard. Susan pushed open the door to her house, went inside, and threw her books onto the bench in the hallway.

Before she could run up to her room to change, her mother rushed into the hallway. She told Susan that they were meeting her father at his office and then going out to dinner. Susan tried to protest, but it did her no good. Ten minutes later, she was driving downtown with her mother, worrying about when she would go to the cemetery.

They didn't come home until 10:00 that night. Susan went up to her room, put on her pajamas, and nervously stared out the window. The tombstones in the graveyard were bathed in the eerie light of the moon. Susan wondered how she would find the black cat there.

Finally her mother came in to say good night. Susan lay on her bed, waiting for the house to fall silent. When at last everything was quiet, she looked at the clock. It was 11:38.

Susan slipped out of her pajamas and into a T-shirt and jeans. Outside her screen window, the September night was still warm. She picked up the flashlight she used for camping trips and quietly stole down the stairs and out of the house.

Susan crept through the darkness past the rickety old house next to the graveyard and then through the arched entrance to the cemetery. She was afraid to use her flashlight in case someone in a nearby house saw her. The full moon shed enough light on the white gravel path for her to find her way in the dark.

Suddenly the stillness in the cemetery was broken by the weird call of a night bird. Susan froze in her steps. Until now, she had not been afraid. But the call reminded her that other things were out there in the night, watching her. She switched on her flashlight and swung it around it a wide circle. The beam lit up the cold, white marble tombstones around her.

Susan kept walking toward the middle of the cemetery, where the black cat was to be found. The gravel path sloped upward at a slight angle, and soon she found herself standing on a small hill. From the streetlights around the edge of the cemetery, she could tell she was near the center.

Susan shone the beam of the flashlight onto the nearby tombstones. The face of an angel stared back out of the darkness, making her catch her breath in fear. Then she saw it. The black cat was like a dark shadow in the night, crouching on top of a huge, white marble tomb.

Susan made her way on trembling legs over to the statue. The night bird shrieked again, sending a chill through her body. She stood underneath the cat and shone her light on it. The animal was made of smooth black marble, except for its eyes, which were of shining green stones. And around its neck, just as the girl had said, was a leather collar.

Susan climbed onto a step of the white base and read the inscription etched into the marble:

DISTURB NOT THE DEAD

For a second, she wanted to turn and run away, as fast as she could, from the tomb and its warning. But there, only inches from her hand, was the collar she had come to get.

She set down her flashlight beside the cat and reached both hands around its marble neck to unfasten the collar.

She whispered grateful thanks as its buckle came easily undone. But at that very moment, the bell on a nearby church began to strike the midnight hour. It frightened Susan so that she almost dropped the collar. On the fourth stroke of the bell, Susan picked up her flashlight and shone it into the cat's face. To her horror, the green eyes gleamed back at her like a real cat's. On the eighth stroke of the bell, Susan climbed down from the tombstone and heard a wicked hiss come from the statue. On the twelfth stroke of the bell, Susan ran down the gravel path of the graveyard, her heart in her throat and her mind in a frenzy of fear.

The light from the flashlight wavered on the path in front of her as Susan ran away from the black cat. She tried to tell herself that she had imagined the cat's hiss. But then, from behind her, she heard the soft thud of animal paws on the gravel path. And a long, angry hiss sounded through the night air. Susan turned around and saw what she feared. Two big green eyes were following her in the darkness.

Finally Susan reached the entrance to the cemetery. She could see her house ahead. It was only yards away now. She ran faster and faster until she reached the front door. With trembling hands she twisted open the knob and ran inside. She shut the door behind her, double-locked it, and then ran up the stairs, panting with fear.

She slipped into her bedroom and shut the door. From outside her screen window, she could hear a neighbor's dog howling weirdly in the night. Susan looked down at her trembling hands and saw the leather collar. Quickly she went to her dresser, opened the top drawer, and hid the collar inside. Then she put on her pajamas and lay down between the sheets, trembling with exhaustion and fear.

Susan stared out her window at the ghostly shapes of the tombstones in the moonlight. She listened to the dog's weird howl. And finally, after a long time, she fell into a fitful sleep.

Susan woke with a start. She had been having a terrible nightmare. In the dream, a black cat had been sitting on her chest, hissing down at her. Susan opened her eyes and stared into the darkness of her room. Then she remembered the collar. She switched on her lamp and ran to the dresser. Quickly she pulled out the top drawer.

The collar was gone.

Then Susan saw the deep claw marks of a cat on the top of the dresser. She whirled around and saw the big ragged hole torn in her window screen.

And there, on the windowsill outside, she saw the black cat . . . staring back at her with glowing green eyes.

The Wax Museum

"There's nothing to be scared of," the oldest boy in the class said in a bragging voice. "The people are just made of wax, like candles."

Still, the group of boys had slowed down to a shuffling pace, stepping on each other's heels and unconsciously herding together for safety. They were walking through the dimly lit entrance to the wax museum. Mr. Archer, their history teacher, was busy back at the admissions desk paying for their tickets.

"I hear this place has all the murderers in history," one young boy said nervously. "Hitler, even."

An uneasy giggle swept over the group. They had all heard stories about Hitler. What would he look like? Mr. Archer had said the wax figures seemed so real that you sometimes forgot they were wax.

Just as the boys came to a wooden door at the end of the hallway, Mr. Archer hurried up from behind them.

"All right, boys," he said in his deep, official voice. "We're ready to begin our tour. The museum director has agreed to let me take you around — since I've been here so often. Now everyone pair up and stand in a straight line."

There were a few minutes of pushing and shoving as the boys found partners and lined up. Mr. Archer looked over the group and noticed that, as usual, Andrew and Robbie had paired up together. He would have to watch them. But perhaps they would be good today, for once.

"Come along, then," Mr. Archer said importantly, opening the door in front of them to reveal a long, narrow room. An aisle ran down the center of the room, and on both sides were displays of people in historical costumes. The boys slowly filed in, their faces lit with amazement.

"They look so alive . . . it's creepy," a young boy said.

"There's Julius Caesar, being stabbed by

Brutus and his friends," one said, pointing his finger at a group of men in Roman togas.

"Ooh, look at the blood!" another boy said. "It still looks wet!"

Mr. Archer chuckled as the boys broke out of line and scrambled up to see the exhibits. Then he saw Andrew and Robbie standing together by the door, whispering to each other.

"Boys, come on in the room!" he said impatiently.

Andrew and Robbie stopped whispering and obediently walked up to the first exhibit. They stared down at Julius Caesar's body which was covered with knife wounds. Caesar's eyes were staring up at his murderers, and his face was twisted in the agony of death.

"This gives me the creeps," Robbie said.

"Not me. I think it's great." Andrew said. "It's like all these dead people have come alive again."

"You're weird," Robbie said.

"So is the museum," Andrew answered. "I wonder what we could do to add a little more excitement to this place."

Both boys turned to look at Mr. Archer, who was watching them with distrustful eyes.

"Why don't we just look at the exhibits?"

Robbie said, turning away from Caesar's bloody body. "I don't want to get into any trouble here."

Robbie stopped in front of another group of wax figures. In the center was Henry VIII, standing with his hands on his hips and his eyes staring straight ahead. Behind the king stood the wax figure of an executioner holding a double-edged ax in his hands. On the ground below him was the wax figure of Anne Boleyn, one of Henry VIII's wives. She was waiting to have her head chopped off at the orders of her husband, the king.

"Look at that ring on Henry's finger," Andrew whispered. "What a great souvenir it would be."

"Andrew!" Robbie said in a scared whisper. "Don't!"

But Andrew didn't pay any attention to him. He checked to see if Mr. Archer and the other boys were looking. Most of them had walked farther on down the aisle of exhibits. Andrew reached his hand out toward the king's left hand. He touched the cold wax of the fingers. Then he put his fingers around the ring and tugged at it. It slipped down a bit, but got stuck over the finger's waxy knuckle.

"Andrew, Robbie!" Mr. Archer's voice called from down the aisle. "Don't lag behind. Come along."

Andrew quickly pulled his hand away from the ring. He glanced up at the wax image of King Henry's face before leaving. The hard eyes were staring straight at him. They even seemed to follow him as he walked away.

"This place might be getting to me," Andrew said to Robbie. "I thought old Henry looked a little angry."

"You're going to get us into trouble," Robbie mumbled.

Andrew looked at him with a sneer. "You're turning out to be some coward, Robbie. Maybe I should get a new friend."

Robbie shook his head so hard that his glasses almost fell off. Andrew was his only friend. The two boys walked down the aisle to catch up with Mr. Archer and the rest of the class.

"Who knows the name of this great man?" Mr. Archer asked as he pointed toward a short man in military uniform standing in front of a map of Europe. The man had a scowl on his face and one hand pushed inside his jacket front.

"Napoléon Bonaparte, emperor of France," said the smartest boy in the class.

"That's correct," Mr. Archer said, beaming at the boy. "This is Napoléon, the great conquerer of Europe who was finally defeated at Waterloo. Now if you'll move along, we'll visit the more modern exhibits in the next room."

The class followed Mr. Archer through a set of heavy velvet curtains into the next room. Robbie started off after them, but Andrew pulled him back.

"Look what I just found," Andrew said, opening his hand to show Robbie something. Robbie peered down at the shiny piece of metal on his outstretched palm.

"It's a pin. Where did you get it?"

"I found it on the floor at home, just before I came here. I thought — "

"No!" Robbie said. "You can't do that. We'd be arrested. . . ."

"Calm down," Andrew said. "Nobody will ever know. I just want to find out if these things are really made of wax."

Andrew picked up the pin and leaned his long arm over the railing in front of the exhibit of Napoléon. He could just reach the emperor's left shoulder. With a quick jab, he pushed the pin through the costume and into the wax.

Robbie let out a short scream.

"Be quiet! What's the matter with you?" Andrew said, quickly pulling out the pin.

"Napoléon moved. I saw him move," Robbie stammered. "When you stuck that pin in, his face moved like it hurt."

Andrew looked at Robbie in disgust. "I can't believe you're such a coward. Look, you can see the wax on the pin. These people may look real, but they're just wax."

Robbie saw the coating of white wax on the pin. Then he looked again at Napoléon's face and ran off down the aisle to join Mr. Archer. Andrew trailed behind, hiding the pin in his pocket.

Mr. Archer was standing in a large round room that had exhibits all around its edges. He was telling the class a story. Robbie and Andrew just heard the end. " . . . and still today, we think of him as the monster of the twentieth century."

"Hitler," Robbie said and pointed to the man with a short mustache in a brown Nazi uniform.

"All right, boys," Mr. Archer said. "There

are many more interesting exhibits in this room. You can look around and ask me any questions you like." He paused and looked at his watch. "But in half an hour we'll be boarding the bus. I promised that I'd have you back in the school parking lot at three-fifteen."

"I don't have to be back," Andrew whispered to Robbie. "My parents are both away on vacation, and I'm staying at home alone."

"You're lucky your parents trust you," Robbie said.

"Especially since they shouldn't," Andrew added. "Let's take a closer look at Hitler."

The rest of the class was looking at different figures in the modern history room — Winston Churchill, Franklin D. Roosevelt, John F. Kennedy, Mahatma Gandhi, and others. Andrew and Robbie stood alone in front of the exhibit of Adolf Hitler and his Nazi officers.

"Even his mustache looks real," Robbie said, staring at Hitler's short, dark mustache.

"I wonder if it's made of real hair," Andrew said. "Turn around, Robbie, and keep a watch on everybody else. Tell me when they're not looking."

"What are you going to do?" Robbie asked in a worried voice.

"Just be quiet and tell me when nobody is looking," Andrew insisted.

Robbie watched nervously for a few minutes. Finally, the moment came when everyone's back was turned to them.

"Now!" he whispered.

Robbie turned around just as Andrew reached his hand out to Hitler's face and pulled at the hair of his mustache.

"It won't come loose!" Andrew hissed under his breath. He gave another hard tug.

Robbie screamed as Andrew's hand came back holding a small tuft of hair. Everyone in the room turned to stare at them.

"What's going on, boys?" Mr. Archer asked, hurrying over.

"Nothing, nothing, sir," Andrew said, hiding his hand behind his back.

"I thought I saw Hitler's hand move," Robbie stammered.

"He has a wild imagination," Andrew broke in to say.

Mr. Archer looked from Robbie to Andrew to the wax figure of Hitler. "Don't be ridiculous, Robbie, that is just a wax figure." Then he walked away, shaking his head.

"His hand did move, Andrew. . . ." Robbie

whispered in a scared voice. "Just when you pulled part of the mustache out. He started to hit you."

"Sure, Robbie, sure," Andrew said, ignoring his friend. "How do you like my souvenir?" He displayed the tuft of hair in his outstretched hand. "I just wish I had that ring on Henry the Eighth's finger." Suddenly, Andrew's face lit up with a smile. "I know what I'll do. And you've got to help me, Robbie."

"No, Andrew, forget it," Robbie said.

"Come on, all you have to do is tell Mr. Archer that I went home early because I felt sick. My parents aren't home to miss me, and I can spend the night in the museum."

"What!" Robbie said.

"I'm going to spend the night here. Think of all the things I could do with nobody around watching me." Andrew glanced quickly around the room. Then he walked over to a wall that was covered by long, heavy velvet curtains. He pulled the curtains aside and looked behind them.

"There's enough room for me to hide here," he whispered. "All you have to do is cover for me. You decide right now whether or not you're going to be my friend."

"Okay," Robbie said, "okay."

Andrew took a quick look around the room and then slipped behind the curtains. Robbie walked away to join Mr. Archer and tell him the lie.

Andrew woke up with a sudden start. For a moment, he wasn't sure where he was. Then he remembered . . . the wax museum. He was hiding behind the curtains in the wax museum. He must have fallen asleep earlier in the night because the air was so hot and musty. He pulled back the curtains to peer out.

The museum was empty and closed. Only a few security lights shone on the exhibits. Andrew checked his watch. Two minutes after midnight. He wondered what had woken him at this hour. Just then, he heard a tapping of something against wood. He turned to look at the exhibit where Hitler stood. A feeling of sickening horror swept over him.

Hitler was tapping a wooden map pointer against his desk. He was pointing around the room and talking to his officers. Andrew pinched himself hard to make sure he wasn't having a terrible nightmare. Just then, he saw Hitler's dark, beady eyes meet his. Hitler let out a scream and barked orders at his officers. Andrew watched with terror as they all began to move from the exhibit and climb over the railing into the room.

Andrew scrambled to his feet and ran for the exit. He glanced back to see Hitler's angry face sneering at him. There was a red mark on his white face where Andrew had pulled off part of his mustache.

Andrew raced down the narrow hallway through the other exhibits. His heart was pounding wildly, and his brain was slowly turning panicky. He fumbled in his pocket for the tuft of hair that he had pulled from Hitler's face. When he found it, he threw the hair on the floor and stumbled on.

The pounding of the Germans' feet was loud behind him, but Andrew gained distance on them as he turned a corner in the aisle. Then, in front of him, he saw Napoléon. The emperor slowly drew his hand out of his jacket and reached for his sword. Andrew's stomach turned inside him as Napoléon pulled the sword from its sheath and leaped over the railing.

Andrew remembered the pin he had stuck in the wax figure. Only the figure wasn't wax anymore. Napoléon was alive and breathing heavily only a few feet behind him. Andrew could hear the swish of the sword in the air and feel the cool breeze it made on his neck.

In a wild panic, Andrew sped forward down the hallway. He knew that soon he would reach the entrance door to the museum. Perhaps a night guard would be there. Perhaps he could jump through a window to safety. Perhaps this nightmare would end if he could only escape through that wooden door.

Then ahead of him he saw a huge figure step from the shadows. It was Henry VIII. He stood in the middle of the hallway, barring Andrew's path. With a cruel smile on his face, the king pointed a finger at Andrew.

The next morning, Robbie led Mr. Archer and a guard into the museum. Robbie hadn't been able to sleep all night worrying about Andrew. Finally, he had called Mr. Archer and told him what Andrew had done.

The guard flicked on all the lights around the exhibits. Robbie started to rush toward the room at the end of the museum where Andrew had hidden. But when he passed the exhibit with Henry VIII, he saw something that made him stop and scream.

Anne Boleyn was no longer the figure kneeling beneath the executioner's ax. Andrew knelt there instead — his face set in a strange expression of terror. And when Robbie reached out to touch him, he felt only the hard, cold smoothness . . . of wax.

Tailypo

There is a place in the mountains where few humans live. The woods around it are deep and dark. A thick fog often settles along the ridges and in the valleys. And weird creatures are said to prowl the land through the long, lonely nights.

There is one old cabin built in a hollow in the farthest part of the deep, dark woods. A man named Jake had lived there for all of his sixty years. He seldom saw other people, and his only friends were his three hunting dogs. They lived under the porch of his log cabin.

One winter night toward spring, Jake sat by his fireplace staring at the pot of beans simmering on the fire. It had been a hard winter, and Jake's food supply was almost gone. He felt as though his stomach had shrunk to the size of one of those hard beans in the pot. Even his dogs had grown thin and scrawny from hunger.

As Jake reached his spoon toward the pot of beans, he felt a cold draft creep around his neck. It sent a shiver through his body. He wondered where the draft was coming from, for he had sealed up the cabin tight for the winter. But he was too hungry to worry about it. He dipped his spoon into the pot of beans. Before he could eat any, he felt another cold draft blowing across the cabin. This time, it felt like icy claws around his neck. Jake turned away from the fire to look around.

His eyes widened in terror, and he dropped the spoon with a clatter on the floor. Sitting across the cabin from him was the weirdest creature he had ever seen. Its eyes were a bright yellow that seemed to burn from some strange heat. Its head looked like a wolf's except for the ears that stuck up in high points above the leering face. Its body, which was about the size of one of Jake's dogs, was covered with a thick, reddish-brown fur. Then Jake noticed the strangest thing of all. The creature had a long, thick tail that wrapped all the way around its body.

For a minute Jake sat frozen in his chair, and the creature crouched still on the floor. They stared at each other from across the room. Then, in a lightning fast move, Jake lunged for his hunting knife on the table. The creature sprang up and jumped for the hole it had clawed into the cabin wall. The animal was fast, but so was Jake. It was just jumping through the hole as Jake's knife came down at it. With a clean slice, the knife cut off the creature's long, thick tail.

There was a horrible screech that cut through the night air. Then the animal ran off into the deep, dark woods. Jake stared at the thick tail lying on the floor of his cabin. His stomach rumbled with hunger. It was meat, like any other part of an animal, and he hadn't had meat for weeks.

Jake put a big kettle of water onto the fire to boil. Then he cooked the long, thick tail and ate it for his supper. It tasted a bit strange, but there was a lot of it. Jake even fed the scraps that were left to his three dogs. As he watched them eat, he thought of the weird creature again. He decided to keep his dogs with him in the cabin for the night.

Before he went to bed, Jake plugged up the hole in the cabin wall with a piece of wood and rags. Then he settled down to sleep, with his three dogs under his bed.

Even though he was exhausted, Jake couldn't go to sleep. His stomach was rumbling from the strange meal. And the wind had picked up outside and was whistling around the cabin.

Then Jake heard a scratching noise outside his door. It was the sound of claws scraping against the wood. And over the whistling of the wind, he heard a weird voice calling, "Tailypo, Tailypo, give me back my Tailypo."

Jake bolted upright in bed. The claws were scratching on the door even louder. And again he heard the weird call, "Tailypo, Tailypo, give me back my Tailypo."

The dogs under his bed began to growl, and Jake whistled them out. He rushed to the cabin door, threw it open, and sent the dogs out after the creature.

There were terrible screeches and howls as the dogs chased the creature into the dark woods. Jake waited and listened. After ten minutes, two of the dogs came panting back to the cabin. But no matter how hard Jack called, the third dog never returned from the woods.

Jake bolted the door and went back to bed with the two dogs lying underneath him. Again his stomach rumbled from his strange meal, and the wind whistled around the cabin.

Then Jake heard a scratching noise outside his door. It was the sound of claws scraping against the wood. And the weird voice started up again, "Tailypo, Tailypo, give me back my Tailypo."

Jake shrunk back into the bed and covered his head with a blanket. But the weird voice came even louder. "Tailypo, Tailypo, give me back my Tailypo. You have got it; that I know. Give me back my Tailypo."

The two dogs under the bed were growling, and Jake whistled them out. Again he threw open the door, and the dogs went bounding out after the creature.

With loud screeching and howling, the dogs chased the animal into the woods. Jake waited and listened. Soon he saw just one dog running back to the cabin in the moonlight. The dog whimpered as Jake let it in the door; then it ran under the bed and hid.

Jake bolted the door and crawled in bed. But he hadn't even shut his eyes before he heard the scratching of claws on the door. And the weird voice said, "Tailypo, Tailypo, give me back my Tailypo."

Jake jumped out of bed and whistled for his last dog. It growled from under the bed and wouldn't come out. Finally Jake dragged it out and pulled it to the door. He opened the door and forced the dog out after the creature.

There was a short howl and then a long screech. Jake waited and listened. After ten minutes, he opened the door and called for the dog. But nothing came back out of the dark woods around the cabin.

Jake slammed the door shut quickly, bolted it, and jumped into his bed. He was shivering hard, but the blankets didn't seem to make him warmer. He waited and waited. The wind whistled louder around the cabin. Jake strained his ears to hear the sound of claws scratching on the door. He waited for the weird voice. He heard nothing but the sound of the wind. Jake waited and listened. Then finally he fell asleep.

With a start, Jake woke up. He heard the sound of claws scratching against wood. But this time, the sound was closer and louder.

Jake's eyes flew open and met the burning yellow eyes staring at him from the end of his bed. The creature sat there, scratching its claws against the bedpost.

"Tailypo, Tailypo, give me back my Tailypo," it said in its weird voice.

"I . . . I . . . don't have it," Jake stammered.

The creature crawled forward on the bed. Its face was only a foot from Jake's.

"Tailypo, Tailypo, give me back my Tailypo. You have got it; that I know. Give me back my Tailypo!"

Jake was never seen in the hills again. And the mountain folk say that if you are all alone at night and listen carefully, you can hear a weird voice calling on the wind:

"Tailypo, Tailypo, now I have my Tailypo!"

Words of Warning

Peter had been in Greenfield for only one day when he heard the story. The old man who told it to him had acted strange, but the story was stranger yet. Peter didn't believe in things like ghosts or haunted houses . . . but it gave him the creeps to think about them.

The old man, whose name was Charlie, had warned him not to go near an abandoned house that was nearby. In the past five years, five boys and girls had last been seen walking toward it. They had disappeared into thin air. The only explanation was that the house was possessed by some strange power.

Peter stood on the porch of the country inn where his family was staying, and he wished that he were home. His parents had driven for hours out of the city to spend the autumn week-end here. They had come to see the fall leaves that turned spectacular colors in this remote part of New England.

Peter was already bored by looking at the leaves, and he couldn't get his mind off Charlie's strange story. Charlie was the gardener for the inn. He said that he'd noticed Peter's hair right away when he had arrived at the inn. That had made Peter uncomfortable, because he didn't like people noticing his red hair.

Charlie said he didn't warn every boy or girl who stopped at the inn about the story, but he felt obliged to tell Peter. The owners of the inn refused to talk about the five boys and girls who had disappeared. They worried that it would be bad for business.

Peter decided he couldn't stand around another second. He ran down the steps of the porch and started down the driveway leading away from the inn. He knew his parents wouldn't miss him. They had left the inn an hour ago to take a walk in the woods. They had carried along their binoculars just in case they sighted an interesting bird. Peter had turned down their invitation to join them. He wasn't interested in bird-watching, and he didn't care about the red, orange, and yellow leaves he was kicking as he walked down the lane.

Several yards ahead, Peter saw a fork in the road. The way leading off to the left was the more traveled road that his father had driven down as they came up to the inn. The way to the right narrowed down to a footpath through a thick stand of trees. A slight tingle ran down Peter's spine as he realized his mind was made up. He was going to take the path to the right, the path that led to the old house that Charlie had told him to stay away from.

As Peter walked down the path, he noticed that the leaves covering it looked undisturbed, as if no one had walked there before him. Yet the path was easy to follow as it cut through the trees and thick undergrowth on the forest floor. Peter suddenly got an eerie feeling at the back of his neck and turned quickly around. But the only thing he saw was a pair of red leaves drifting slowly down to the ground.

Peter walked on for fifteen minutes, looking ahead and seeing nothing but more trees. He began to wonder if the old man had played a joke on him, a kid from the city. But then he came to a wide clearing in the trees, and standing there, like a scene from a horror movie, was a gray-shingled, dilapidated house.

A whirlwind of leaves suddenly blew around in front of Peter as a cloud passed over the sun. The colors of the leaves faded without the sunlight, and the house seemed to cast a shadow over everything around it.

Peter pushed back the feeling of panic that had started growing in his mind. He took a few more steps toward the house. It was an old, rambling, three-story structure with a porch all around it. Many of its windows were broken. The porch sagged at a sickening angle, and the shutters hung crookedly on their hinges.

Peter thought about his friends back home. They would love hearing his story about this house. But they would ask if he'd gone inside. And if he said no, they would call him a chicken.

Peter tried not to think too much and began to walk up to the house with quick strides. But the old man's story kept coming back into his mind. The strange story seemed more real now that he was standing in front of the house. He hesitated before setting his foot on the first step of the stairs leading up to the porch.

The wind had died down and there wasn't a sound except the occasional call of a bird in the woods. Peter stood there, undecided. He heard a faint noise inside the house. It grew a little louder, a strange kind of noise he'd never heard before. Then a weird sensation came over him. He felt drawn toward the house as though something were pulling him inside. Unwillingly, his right foot went forward and stepped up onto the first step. Peter screamed and pulled his body back. He scrambled back from whatever power had come over him and ran into the woods. He tore along the path, bumping into trees and scratching himself on branches. Ten minutes later, he ran up to the inn, where his mother and father were sitting on the porch.

"Peter, what happened?" his mother asked.

"Nothing," Peter gasped, his heart pounding in his ears, "just nothing."

The next day, more guests arrived at the inn. Peter sat on the porch and watched them as they unpacked their cars and settled in. One family had two boys near his age. They came out on the porch and introduced themselves right away. Brian, who was tall and skinny and had dark brown hair, was fourteen. Jeff, who was short and stocky and had blond hair, was twelve. Peter noticed the old gardener Charlie staring at them from the yard, but he just kept raking leaves.

"So, what's there to do around here?" Jeff said. "My parents brought us up here to look at leaves. So here are the leaves. What do we do now?"

"There isn't even a television in our room," Brian said. "I can't believe we're stuck here for a whole weekend."

"What have you been doing?" Jeff asked. "Watching birds?"

Peter sat up straight. He could tell them something exciting.

"I went to a haunted house yesterday," he said. "It's not far from here — and it's really creepy."

Jeff let out a high-pitched laugh. "You believe in haunted houses? I can't take it!"

Peter felt a blush creeping over his face. "I'll show you where it is," he said. "You can see for yourself."

"Great, we'll meet you on the front steps in half an hour," Brain said. "Right after we unpack."

"In half an hour," Peter repeated. As they walked away, he looked out at Charlie raking the leaves. He wondered why Charlie hadn't warned Jeff and Brian about the house.

Half an hour later, Peter stood waiting by the front steps of the inn. He kicked a pile of leaves impatiently, wondering if Jeff and Brian would show up. He wished they would hurry. If Charlie happened to come around to the front, Peter didn't want him to see them going off in the direction of the old house.

Finally the screen door of the inn slammed loudly and Jeff and Brian bounded down the steps at a run.

"Lead the way," they yelled to Peter.

The three boys ran off down the land and, at the fork, took the path to the right that led to the old house. Peter was running in the lead, with the two boys close behind him. As the path grew more narrow, they slowed their pace to a walk.

"Were you kidding us about this house?" Jeff asked as they walked through the carpet of leaves that had grown even thicker.

"It's here, all right," Peter said. He knew the house was only a few minutes away, because his chest had started to grow heavy with anxiety.

Soon they walked out into the clearing

around the house. Peter looked at the house, hulking like a dark giant among the brightly colored trees, and shuddered.

"Wow," Jeff whispered. "It looks haunted all right!"

"Let's go," Brian yelled, starting toward the house at a run. Jeff ran quickly after him.

"No, wait!" Peter screamed. He stayed where he was at the edge of the clearing. The other boys turned around and stared at him.

"What's the matter with you?" Jeff asked. "Are you chicken?"

"I wouldn't go any farther if I were you," Peter warned.

The two boys laughed at him and ran up to the house. Peter watched as they bounded up the porch stairs two at a time. Brian reached the door first. He grabbed the old handle and gave it a hard push. The door swung open with a sickening creak.

Peter took a few steps closer to the house. Brian and Jeff looked back at him and laughed again. Then they both went inside the house. Peter felt a sweat break out on his brow. He couldn't bring himself to go up to the house, no matter how he willed his feet to move forward.

Ten minutes later, Brian and Jeff came out

of the house covered with dust and cobwebs.

"Some haunted house," Jeff said. "All that's in there is a bunch of old furniture."

"Why didn't you come in?" Brian asked. "You're not really afraid of that place, are you?"

"Come on, I've got to get back," Peter said, starting off down the path to the inn.

"Chicken," Jeff whispered behind his back.

"Chicken," Brian echoed.

The next day Jeff and Brian ignored Peter. He knew what they thought of him. And he was beginning to think they were right. Why should he be afraid of the old house if the two of them had walked around inside it and not seen or heard a thing? He had just let the old man's story get to his imagination.

Peter nervously ran his hand through his red hair. Then he made up his mind. He was going back to the house. He would prove to himself that he wasn't a chicken. And he would come back and tell Jeff and Brian what he'd done. Maybe he could even bring something back from inside to prove it.

Peter looked up as he set off from the inn. Storm clouds were gathering in the late afternoon sky. A chilling autumn wind cut through his sweater and blew the leaves off the trees in swirling clumps. The path leading to the old house looked different today. Many of the trees along it had been stripped almost bare of their leaves. The white birches looked like skeletons shivering in the wind. Peter stuck his hands in his pockets and kicked fiercely through the leaves at his feet. Why had Charlie ever told him that story anyway?

Peter started to run along the path to warm himself up. The sooner he got to the house, the sooner it would be over. Within a short time, he was standing at the clearing with the house in front of him.

Just like yesterday, he found that his legs were suddenly frozen with fear. The house looked evil today, hunched under the dark gray sky. Peter forced himself to walk toward it. He hugged his arms around his body, trying to keep himself from shaking. Step by step, he drew nearer to the stairs going up to the front porch.

The old man's words of warning went through his mind, but Peter ignored them. He couldn't stop now. A step away from the stairs, he heard the same weird, whooshing noise he'd heard before. A swell of panic rose inside him. He tried to stop his foot from stepping onto the first stair. But it was too late. Just then, two invisible arms grabbed hold of him and pulled him up the stairs onto the porch. And then, in front of him, the door to the house swung open as if pushed by an invisible hand.

Peter felt himself being pulled inside the house. He couldn't run away. He couldn't escape. The door slammed behind him.

Peter looked around the room in terror. Five ghostly faces stared back at him. And finally, Peter understood the old man's words of warning . . . for each ghost had red hair.

The Ghost's Revenge

The young Confederate soldiers marched along the road, their bodies exhausted from battle, their uniforms bloody and torn. But they were the lucky ones. They had survived the awful battle that the Union soldiers had won. Many of their friends lay dead on the battlefield, never to return.

A young lieutenant named William Compton rode his horse alongside them. It had been his first battle, and he had seen things he wanted to forget. Several times, he had smelled death lurking near him, but he had escaped. William looked up from the dusty road to see a carriage passing by the line of soldiers. A pretty young girl sat in it. She met his eyes and smiled.

Inside the carriage, Lucy Potter continued

to smile. The young officer had looked dirty and tired, but he was very handsome. Like many young men, he obviously found her lovely to look at. Lucy had just turned seventeen, and she spent a great deal of time in front of the mirror.

The carriage jolted on down the rough road, carrying Lucy to her uncle's plantation in the country. She had had to flee from the city where she was going to a boarding school when the Union soldiers had drawn too near. Her rich uncle had offered to take her in, since she had been orphaned three years ago when both her parents had died in an epidemic.

Lucy stuck her head out the carriage window to peer back at the soldiers. The war was exciting to her, and she thought the young men looked brave and dashing in their uniforms. Someday soon she hoped to meet a handsome, rich man and marry him.

The shadows of night were falling over the white-columned mansion when Lucy arrived at her uncle's house. It was a beautiful, spacious house — very different from the modest home Lucy had grown up in. As she walked up to the door held open by a servant, she vowed to live this life always. She must simply marry the right husband.

Lucy's aunt and uncle received her with affection and hospitality. She was shown to a beautiful bedroom with a closet full of expensive dresses that had belonged to her cousin Eleanor, who had died in the same epidemic as Lucy's parents. Before she went to bed, Lucy tried many of the dresses on. She looked in the mirror and smiled. Her new life was beginning.

In the middle of that night, a knock sounded on the mansion door. Lucy's uncle, Thomas Potter, opened it and saw an exhausted Confederate captain standing there. The officer asked if his soldiers could spend the night on Mr. Potter's land. Mr. Potter readily agreed and invited the officer and his lieutenants to stay in the mansion.

Lucy came down for breakfast the next morning dressed in a rose-colored silk dress that cast a glow over her white skin and set off her deep blue eyes. She walked into the dining room, expecting to greet only her aunt and uncle. She was startled to see four young men and one older man sitting with her relatives. They were all dressed in the gray uniforms of officers of the Confederate army.

"My niece, Lucy Potter," her uncle said graciously. Then, as all the officers rose to meet her, he introduced each of them. Lucy nodded and smiled to each. But she smiled most when she was introduced to Lieutenant William Compton. She remembered having seen his handsome face from her carriage the day before. Today it was scrubbed clean and his auburn hair shone in the sunlight. She took her place across from his at the long table set with fine china and silver.

During the breakfast, while Mr. Potter and the officers discussed the progress of the war, Lucy often looked up to see William Compton staring at her with a longing look in his brown eyes. She let herself blush, knowing it complimented her.

"I insist that you and your men stay on the plantation until you get further orders," Mr. Potter said to the captain.

"Thank you, sir," the captain answered. "My men need to stop running for a while. The war has taken its toll on them."

Lucy looked again at Lieutenant Compton and saw the happiness on his face. She wondered if he was as rich as he was handsome. She vowed to find out as soon as possible.

That afternoon, from her bedroom window, Lucy saw Lieutenant Compton walking in the rose garden near the mansion. She look a last look in the mirror, then hurried down the wide staircase, out the door of the mansion, and down the path to the rose garden. She slowed down when she saw the lieutenant leaning against an old oak ahead.

"Lucy," he said with more feeling than he wanted to betray when he saw her. "Excuse me, I mean Miss Potter."

She insisted that he call her Lucy, and he asked that she call him William. By the time they had walked around the rose garden twice, she knew that he was in love with her. War had brought his feelings close to the surface and made them intense.

Once he started to tell her about the terrible battle he'd just been in, but then stopped. He turned away and broke off a red rose from a nearby bush. He picked off the thorns and gave it to Lucy with a look that made her heart pound.

That evening they sat beside each other at dinner and shared private conversation while the others talked about Mr. Lincoln and the war. Lucy went to bed that night with her head swimming with thoughts of William. She reminded herself that tomorrow she must find out how rich he was.

The next evening, as they sat together in the rose garden after dinner, Lucy asked William where his home was. But instead of hearing about a white mansion like her uncle's, she heard about a wood-frame house like the one she had grown up in. Her heart sank as she listened to him speak sadly of his widowed mother, living a life made poorer by the war. But his words faded from her mind when he kissed her under a tree in the shadows of the Spanish moss that hung like a canopy around them.

The soldiers stayed on for three more weeks while General Lee planned his next move against the Union army. Lucy and William spent their days together and dreamed of each other at night. Then one morning the captain made an announcement at breakfast.

"Tomorrow we march north," he said. "The Union army is on the move again. We'll meet them in battle fifty miles north of here."

Lucy met William's eyes and saw the shudder pass through his body. The captain gave orders to his lieutenants about all they had to do that day. Before he left, William made Lucy promise to meet him in the rose garden that night.

They met under the same tree as before. Lucy's heart beat fast as she watched William pull out something small and shiny from the pocket of his uniform. Then she felt him slip the smooth, gold band onto the ring finger of her left hand.

"Marry me, Lucy, when I come back," he said, dropping down on one knee as he asked her.

Lucy looked at the plain ring in the moonlight. She had always dreamed of a diamond ring, a huge stone that sent off glints of fire. But then she looked down at William's face. He was going off to battle the next day. She said she would marry him.

William stood up and kissed her. Then he held her shoulders tightly in his hands and stared intently into her eyes. "Promise me something, Lucy," he asked. "If I don't come back from this battle, say you'll never marry anyone else."

Lucy hesitated. She twisted the tight ring

around her finger. William was still staring into her eyes. "I promise, William. I'll never marry anyone but you."

The soldiers left the next morning. William rode away on his horse, waving good-bye to Lucy on the steps of the mansion. Lucy nervously twisted the ring on her finger as she watched him until he rode out of sight. Then she went up to her room and stared in the mirror.

Five nights later, there was another knock on the mansion door. Again Mr. Potter opened it to find an exhausted Confederate officer. He was a young captain with news of the terrible battle that had taken place fifty miles to the north. The South had lost the battle and suffered a great loss of men. Captain Sanders asked if he and his men could stay on Mr. Potter's land. Before he left to settle in his men, he gave one more piece of news. Another captain had told him to bring news about Lieutenant William Compton to Miss Lucy Potter. Lieutenant Compton had been shot in the battle and was dead.

When Mr. Potter broke the news to Lucy the next morning, he waited for her to cry. But she seemed to take William's death with great calm. She only betrayed her feelings by twisting the gold ring around her finger over and over again.

The next weeks were confused and chaotic in the mansion. The young captain had moved into the house with his other officers. The servants and family tended to the sick and wounded soldiers quartered in the barns. Lucy found that the memories of William that haunted her were eased by the presence of Captain Sanders. She found him handsome and was fascinated by the stories he told of his father's plantation, which was still prosperous and safe in the Deep South. Lucy suspected that Captain Sanders found her attractive, but he was too much of a gentleman to show it, especially since he had brought the news of her fiance's death.

One day Captain Sanders offered to take her to the cemetery where the Confederate soldiers killed in the great battle had been buried. Lieutenant Compton was among them. Lucy eagerly accepted his invitation, and when the day came, she chose to wear a brightly colored dress that complimented her. She rode in the carriage with the captain to the cemetery, nervously twisting the gold band around her finger as she listened to his stories of his life before the war.

When the captain took her to William's grave, she insisted that she be left alone there. And when she saw that Captain Sanders was out of sight, she pulled the gold ring off her finger and threw it among the weeds that had already sprung up over William's grave.

Her aunt and uncle were shocked when, two months later, Captain Sanders announced that Lucy had agreed to marry him. They were both eager to be married before the next great battle. Hastily, Mr. Potter arranged for the wedding to take place the next Saturday in the local church.

Lucy walked around the mansion as if on air, showing everyone the beautiful diamond engagement ring that Captain Sanders had given her. The best seamstress in the county was hired to work day and night to make a beautiful silk and lace wedding gown. Only once did her aunt dare to mention William Compton's name. Lucy had screamed that she never wanted to hear of him again, and she had twisted the diamond ring on her finger so hard that she cut herself.

On the morning of her wedding, Lucy walked down the aisle of the small country church on the arm of her uncle. She stared lovingly into the eyes of her bridegroom as he waited for her at the altar.

The minister began the ceremony. As she came closer and closer to the moment when she would become Captain Sander's rich and beautiful wife, Lucy felt a nervousness rising inside her. The ring on her finger seemed to be burning with unnatural heat, and Lucy had to hold herself back from twisting it around and around.

The minister came to the familiar words of the wedding ceremony, just before he pronounced them man and wife. "If anyone has cause to stop this marriage, let him speak now . . . or forever hold his peace."

Lucy felt a horrible coldness start at the back of her neck and then creep all through her body. Then she heard the bang of a door and felt a cold wind rush up the aisle. Like everyone else in the church, she turned around. She met the gaze of William Compton, standing at the back of the church.

As he walked, step by step, up the aisle toward her, Lucy saw the red stain on his gray uniform. It looked like a red rose over his heart. But as he came closer and closer, she saw that it was blood.

William's eyes burned like fire, but his face was the horrible white of death. Lucy shrank back and clasped her right hand over the diamond ring to hide it. Everyone else seemed frozen by the cold, cold wind that blew through the church like a whirlwind with William at its center.

Lucy screamed in horror as she saw William's white, bony hands reach out toward her. Then she felt herself being swooped up in a deathly grip and carried down the aisle by her ghostly bridegroom.

When Captain Sanders and Lucy's relatives rushed out of the church, they could find no sign of Lucy. They only heard the eerie clip-clopping of a horse's hoofs breaking into a gallop.

The men called for their horses and rode off in the direction of the sound the horse had taken. They galloped down the road that led inevitably to the graveyard where William

Compton had been laid to his uneasy rest. Captain Sanders ran through the tombstones to the place where he had brought Lucy only a short time before.

The weeds had grown higher on the grave. Lucy lay dead among them, her hands clutching the tombstone. And on the third finger of her left hand was the plain gold ring . . . that William Compton had given his bride.

A Special Treat

It was exactly one year since Lisa and Harry had been married. For their first anniversary, Lisa prepared a meal that she knew Harry would love. As she stood in the kitchen, ready to serve the first course, Lisa ran through the menu in her mind. Cream of broccoli soup. Stuffed mushrooms. Baked trout Florentine. Potatoes au gratin. Tossed salad. Chocolate mousse.

Then Lisa sighed. Of course, there was no red meat. Red meat was not allowed.

Harry's face broke into a smile as Lisa brought in the soup. They sat down, wished each other a happy anniversary, and began to eat. Lisa watched her husband with adoring eyes. She thought he was very handsome, even though her parents thought he should trim his full beard and thick hair.

As they ate one course after another, Harry complimented Lisa on each dish. He finished off the dessert of chocolate mousse with a satisfied sigh. "I'm the luckiest man in the world," he said, smiling at Lisa. "You're a wonderful cook."

"Thank you," Lisa said. Then she quickly added, "Perhaps I could make you a steak, or even just a hamburger, some night."

"Lisa," Harry said sternly. "You know I cannot eat red meat."

"But Harry . . ." Lisa began weakly. She knew it was going to be a hopeless argument.

"My mother said I should never eat red meat," Harry said firmly. "You know that, Lisa. We needn't discuss it further." He got up from his chair and began to clear the table.

"Why should you still do what your mother told you, Harry? You haven't seen her for twenty years."

"During the five years that my mother was at home, I never ate red meat," Harry replied. "And the last words my mother said to me — just as she was running wildly out the door — were: 'Never eat red meat!' "

Lisa decided to drop the subject. After all, it was their anniversary.

But during the next week, Lisa found herself dwelling on Harry's stubbornness each time she cooked a meal. She liked red meat. It wasn't fair to her that she could never enjoy pot roast or leg of lamb or pork chops. Resentment against Harry's mother seethed and grew inside her. His mother must have been crazy, Lisa thought, to run out on Harry and her husband and never come back.

Harry didn't like to talk about his mother, but Lisa brought up the subject one night over a dinner of eggplant lasagna, a meatless dish that Harry loved.

"What sort of food did your mother cook for you, Harry?" Lisa asked calmly.

Harry looked up from his food with a surprised expression on his face. "You know I don't like thinking about my mother, Lisa," he said. "But now that you've brought it up, she made tuna noodle casserole."

"What else?" Lisa asked.

"That's all I remember, tuna noodle casserole," Harry said defensively. "Now can we drop the subject, please."

From that night on, a plan began to form in

Lisa's mind. She would help Harry get over his irrational fear of red meat. His mother had obviously been neurotic, and she had passed on her ridiculous ideas to her son.

Lisa began to study her cookbooks. She needed to find a recipe that changed the texture and appearance of red meat enough to fool Harry. Finally she found something called Noodle Surprise. The main ingredient was noodles in a thick cream sauce spiced with paprika. But hidden in the cream sauce was finely chopped red meat. Lisa put a piece of paper in the book to mark the place. And then she smiled, trying to imagine Harry's surprise when he found out what he had eaten in Noodle Surprise.

Lisa had to wait another week until the right day came for her experiment. One day Harry announced that he would have to work longer than usual the next evening, but he would be home in time for a late dinner. Lisa assured him with a smile that his meal would be waiting when he got home.

The next afternoon, Lisa went to the supermarket and ran up to the meat counter. "One pound of your best beef for roasting," she told the butcher.

She watched as the butcher reached for a

tray of red meat in the display case. Lisa had never seen such red meat. The butcher cut off a large piece, weighed it, and wrapped it up. Lisa gently put it into her shopping cart as though it were precious caviar.

Late that afternoon, she roasted the meat until it was tenderly done. Then she chopped it into fine pieces, stirred it into the cream sauce for Noodle Surprise, and put the dish in the oven to bake. She was just pulling the casserole out of the oven when she felt a kiss on the back of her neck.

Lisa screamed and almost dropped the food. She whirled around to see Harry smiling at her.

"It's only me," he said and then stared at the expression on her face. "Why do you look guilty?"

"Guilty?" Lisa said, setting down the Noodle Surprise. "Don't be silly. I was just hoping to have dinner on the table when you came home."

"What did you make?" Harry asked.

"A special treat," Lisa answered.

She brought the casserole of Noodle Surprise into the dining room and set it down in the middle of the table.

"Lisa, your hands are shaking," Harry said

as she spooned a large serving on his plate. "Did you have a hard day?"

"Not really," Lisa said, putting some Noodle Surprise on her plate. "How was your day?"

She asked Harry question after question to keep him from looking too closely at the food on his plate. Finally he took his first bite. Lisa held her breath as she watched him chew and swallow it.

"Lisa," he asked. "What's that strange taste in this food?"

Lisa's heart began to pound. "Paprika," she answered.

"No, it's not the paprika," Harry said. "It's something else. I've never tasted it before." Harry took another forkful of the casserole and hungrily ate it. "Delicious!" he said with his mouth full.

Lisa had to hide her smile behind her napkin as she watched Harry wolf down the food. She had never seen him eat so greedily.

"More!" Harry demanded, pushing his plate out to her.

"Harry, remember your manners," Lisa said, putting another huge serving on his plate.

A strange sound came from low in Harry's

throat as he began to eat the second helping. Lisa looked up in alarm.

"Harry, did your stomach just growl?" she asked.

Harry didn't answer. He finished the last forkful of food on his plate and pushed it across the table toward her.

"More," he said again, but his voice sounded so strange that Lisa hardly recognized it.

"Harry, really, I don't know what's come over you," Lisa said nervously, serving him more Noodle Surprise.

"I . . . love . . . this . . . food," Harry said in the strange voice. Then he reached his hand out to pull back his plate.

Lisa screamed. Harry's hand was covered with tufts of hair that looked just like his beard. She looked up at his face and saw a strange gleam in his eyes. Harry smiled at her, showing long, pointed teeth.

Lisa screamed again and tried to tug the plate of food away from Harry. He pulled it back away from her.

"No, Harry, no! Don't eat it," she pleaded. "It's red meat!"

For a second, they both froze and stared at each other across the table. Then the doorbell rang. A weird expression came over Harry's face, and he jumped up from the table. Lisa rushed after him to the front door. Then she screamed as Harry flung the door open.

A creature stood there smiling at Harry. She had graying hair all over her body.

"Mother!" Harry growled.

"Harry," the werewolf growled back.

Then, together, they ran wildly out into the night.

Lisa stood in the doorway, staring up at the full moon in the dark sky. She heard the sound of two howls echoing together through the night. Then she walked back into the dining room and sat down, alone.

She knew she would never see Harry again. And she knew that she would never, ever eat red meat.

The Magic Vanishing Box

Ben had wandered into a part of the city that
he'd never seen before. The streets were lined
with antique shops and second-hand stores. As
he passed by one old shop, Ben stopped to look
at a display in its window. Sitting in the midst
of other antiques was a tattered, black top hat
with an old stuffed rabbit popping out of it.

Ben wondered if it was a real magician's hat.
Magic was his hobby. It was almost an obses-
sion with him, in fact. He read everything he
could about it and practiced tricks in his spare
time.

Ben went to the shop door and read the sign:
Curiosities of the Past. He pushed open the
door and went inside. One glance around the
small one-room shop told him it lived up to its

name. There were stuffed monkeys sitting beside huge brass candlesticks. There were life-size china dogs sitting on carved wooden boxes that looked like coffins. The shop was very curious, indeed.

Ben began to look through the knicknacks and larger items displayed on the tables and shelves in the room.

"May I help you?"

Ben whirled around at the sound of the voice. He saw a stooped old man looking at him with piercing eyes.

"I . . . I was just looking around," Ben stammered.

"Take your time, take your time," the man said. "I'll be in the back if you need me. Ring this bell if you want to buy anything." The man gestured to an old brass bell by the cash register and then hobbled off into the back of the store.

Ben shrugged his shoulders and continued to walk around the store. He took a closer look at the silk top hat in the window. It was a magician's hat, but he had no need for another one. Ben wondered if there might be other magic tricks in the store, old ones that he'd never seen before.

For half an hour Ben lost track of the time as he searched through the jumble of odds and ends on display. Then something caught his eye. It was a shiny, black wood box about two feet square. Ben ran his hand over the smooth wood, the brass hinge at the front, and the brass-covered corners.

But what interested him most was the little brass plate on top of the box. It was engraved with the words: *The Magic Vanishing Box.* With care, Ben unlatched the brass hinge at the front of the box and lifted the lid. Inside, there was nothing, just the empty interior of the black wood. Then Ben caught sight of another brass plate on the inside of the lid. It, too, was engraved with words: *Don't catch your hand inside this lid, or else you'll be sorry that you did.*

Ben carefully shut the lid on the box and stared at it for a long time. What was a magic vanishing box? It was probably some sort of joke. Still, Ben wanted it more than he'd wanted anything for a long time. He reached in his pocket to check the money he'd brought along for his trip into the city. Fifteen dollars. And he needed two dollars of that to get home.

All he had to spend on the box was thirteen dollars.

Ben picked up the box and carried it over to the counter by the cash register. He pressed his hand down on the bell. A shrill ding echoed through the store. Soon the old man came out from the back room. He looked at Ben; then he looked at the box. Slowly a strange smile spread over his face.

An hour later, Ben was in his bedroom unwrapping the newspaper that the old man had bundled around the box. His hands were trembling as he set the shiny box on top of his desk. Again he read the words on the brass plate: *The Magic Vanishing Box.* Ben decided he couldn't wait any longer. He had to find out if he had spent his thirteen dollars foolishly. Carefully he opened the lid to the box and looked inside. There were no instructions except for the warning he'd read before: *Don't catch your hand inside this lid, or else you'll be sorry that you did.*

Ben gingerly opened the lid all the way and then looked around the room. What could he experiment with first? His eyes fell on the blue dictionary that sat on his desk. It would just fit into the box, and he wouldn't care in the least if it vanished.

Ben picked up the heavy book and set it into the bottom of the box. Then he cautiously closed the lid by holding on to its front brass hinge. He felt silly about taking the warning inside the box seriously. After all, it was probably just a practical joke. He snapped down the hinge into place and stood staring at the box. There were no magic words to say; no magic wand to wave. Ben waited for a few minutes, then he opened the lid.

The inside of the box was empty.

Ben stared at the empty, black space for a moment, then he picked up the box to look under it. Nothing was there. Carefully, he shut the lid and turned the box over and over, looking for the secret to its magic. He knew there must be a trick. Things didn't just vanish.

At last he found what he was looking for. On one side of the box, right beside the brass corner decoration, was a small brass latch. Ben pulled it until it sprung; then a tiny drawer shot open from the side of the box.

Ben stared down at the weird things inside

the drawer. There was a tiny blue book lying beside a small, life-like figure of a boy. Ben picked up the book first. He squinted to read the small print of the title. It was a dictionary, a perfect miniature version of his dictionary. He flipped through the pages, and then suddenly let it drop as though it had burned him. How had the box done that? What kind of magic did it have?

Ben's eyes were drawn to the small figure of the boy. It was only about two inches high and was dressed in old-fashioned clothes. The details of its face and clothing were so realistic that it could have been alive, except that it was so small.

Ben set the tiny book and the figure on his bookshelf. Then he shut the secret drawer, opened the box lid, and looked around his room for something else to test. He still couldn't believe this was happening to him.

He caught sight of his face in the mirror above his dresser. The freckles on his face were standing out against his white skin. He pinched his arm under his red football jersey, just to make sure he was awake. The box was the strangest trick he had ever used. And there was something even more strange. It didn't seem to be just a trick — it was real magic.

Ben picked up a pencil, put it in the box, and shut the lid. A minute later, he pushed the latch on the secret drawer. It shot open, and inside was a perfect replica of the pencil, so little that Ben could hardly pick it up.

Ben looked at the clock in his room. He knew his parents would be home soon, and he wanted to keep the box a secret. But he had to try the trick just one more time. This time he would put in something unusual. He looked up and saw his transistor radio. Would the radio still be able to play music if it were turned into a miniature?

Ben opened the lid of the box and reached up for his radio. It just fit inside the box. As he started to close the lid, Ben saw that the radio's antenna was sticking up. He reached one hand inside the box to push the antenna down.

Just then his mother's voice called from downstairs, "Ben, we're home."

Ben swung his head around in panic. Then the heavy, black lid of the box slammed down on his hand. For a second it hurt. Then Ben felt nothing.

* * *

For a year the police searched for Ben. But the only clues they had to work with were the strange black box and the tiny book and figure they found in his room. Finally the police gave up. Ben's parents cleaned out his room and gave away his belongings. And eventually the black box made its way back to the old antique shop where Ben had bought it.

The old man sat it back on its shelf. It waited there for another boy to come in and buy it. And that boy would find its secret drawer — and, inside the drawer, a small life-like figure of a boy with freckles wearing a red football jersey.

Wait Till Max Comes

One dark and stormy night, a stranger walked down a lonely road between two villages. He had traveled for several miles without seeing a house, and he was growing more and more worried about the weather.

A cold wind had sprung up, whipping the tree branches around and blowing dust into his eyes. The sky was dark with angry thunderclouds, even though sunset was still an hour away. Then a streak of lightning cut through the black clouds, making everything suddenly bright. It was followed by a rumble of thunder that rocked the earth.

The man stopped in his tracks and began to tremble. There was going to be a terrible storm. He had to find shelter.

He peered through the trees that lined both sides of the road, but the light had grown so dim that he could see nothing but shadows. Then another jagged bolt of lightning shot through the sky. The man looked up and saw the silhouette of a house against the sky. It sat on top of a hill above the road.

The man waited, and another flash of lightning came. By its light he saw the entrance to a narrow lane along the road. He stumbled over to it and started to climb the winding path up to the house.

Hard drops of rain splattered down on the man's bare head. The ground beneath his feet became slippery as it grew wetter and wetter. By now the man was panting from trying to run up the hill. He began to doubt whether this lane led to the house at all.

Then suddenly he walked out of the narrow lane and into a clearing. A streak of lightning shot across the sky and lit up a huge house with pointed gables and dark windows that looked like sinister eyes. The man drew back and gasped. The house looked like an evil animal, crouched in the dark. He thought about running back down the lane to the road.

But then the wind sprang up even harder,

whipping the cold rain against the man's body. He ran for the house and found the front door. To his surprise, the latch opened when he tried it. Cautiously he crept inside and shut the door behind him.

The house was as still as a tomb. The man could hear the pounding of the rain outside, but inside all was silent. He fumbled in his pocket and found a match. He struck it, and the burst of flame lit up the hallway he stood in. A pair of candlesticks sat on the table nearby. He lit a candle, picked it up, and began to walk through the house.

The first room he stepped into had a big fireplace with wood stacked in it. The man bent down and lit the wood with his candle flame. Before long, the room was filled with the warm crackle of a burning fire. The man could see the broken-out glass in several of the windows and the thick layer of dust that covered everything in the room.

He sat down in the chair that was pulled up by the fireplace and warmed his cold, weary body. Perhaps he was safe here after all, he thought.

The man had just shut his eyes to sleep when he heard a soft, little cry. He opened his eyes and saw a small, gray kitten sitting on the hearth by the fire. It looked up at him and meowed again.

The kitten made the man feel even more peaceful and secure. Once again, he shut his eyes. Then he heard another cry. This time it was louder and stronger. He opened his eyes and saw a full-grown, striped cat sitting beside the little, gray kitten. Now four green eyes stared back at him from the hearthside.

The man liked cats, so this did not bother him very much. Once again, he shut his eyes.

"What will we do with him?"

The man's eyes flew open. Who had said that? He searched around the room. But he saw only the two cats sitting by the fireplace. It must have been his imagination, he told himself.

Then he saw the striped cat turn to the gray kitten and say, "Wait till Max comes."

The man started to tremble and squeezed his eyes shut. Maybe he was losing his mind. Then he heard another sound, a very loud hiss.

He looked at the hearth and saw a third cat, yellow and as big as a dog, sitting beside the other two.

"What'll we do with him?" the striped cat asked.

"Wait till Max comes," the yellow cat said.

The man began to wonder how fast he could run for the door. But it was too late. Just then, a fourth cat walked into the room. It was as big as a leopard and as black as the night. Its eyes were yellow instead of green and they looked the man over from head to toe.

"What should we do with him?" the yellow cat asked.

"Wait till Max comes," the black cat said. Then it sat down in front of the doorway.

The man looked at the four cats staring at him hungrily. Then he looked over at the window nearest him that had its glass broken out. With one leap, the man sprang from the chair and jumped out the window.

"Tell Max I couldn't wait!" he screamed.

The man ran home, locked himself in his house, and never came out again. For he knew that somewhere, out there, Max was waiting for him.

The Old Beggar Woman

It was a time of hardship and poverty in the villages along the New England coast. The crops had failed, and food was scarce. Beggars, wearing tattered clothes and haunting faces, roamed the countryside asking for food or shelter for the night. Good people shared the little they had with the starving poor. But one person turned away from them and admired her plump image in the mirror.

Mrs. Agatha Parry lived in a splendid mansion on top of a high cliff overlooking the Atlantic Ocean. Her husband had owned a whole fleet of whaling ships and had become rich from the profits of whale oil. Captain Parry had died five years earlier, leaving his widow the richest woman in the county.

Some people said that Agatha Parry had become mean and stingy after her husband's death. Others said she had always been so; her husband had made up for it by his generosity to the poor and unfortunate. Stories and rumors flew around the nearby towns about Agatha Parry. She had nearly starved a maid to death for not polishing the silver well enough. She insisted that leftover food be fed to her lap dogs rather than given to the poor. She wouldn't let beggars come to the mansion doors and made her servants push them away into the dark and cold night.

Agatha Parry seldom went to town. She had everything on her estate that she could wish for. Her mansion was filled with paintings by famous artists. There was a music room with a grand piano and a gold harp. In the dining room Agatha Parry ate at the head of a long table laid with fine china and silver. Her guests, mostly wealthy people from far away, were still not as wealthy as she and greedily ate the delicacies set before them.

If it were not for her daily walk along the cliffs, Agatha Parry would never have seen the poor and starving people who lived around her. But she believed that the sea air was good for her complexion, so she took a walk in the early evening each day. The beggars had become desperate enough to follow the rich lady to the cliffs and beg for food from her there.

After seeing their hollow faces and dirty clothes, Agatha had held her handkerchief to her nose and screamed for her servants. She demanded that the cliffs be cleared of beggars before her walk from then on. She wouldn't have the sight of these horrid people spoiling her complexion.

One evening, as usual, Agatha set off from her mansion for her walk on the cliffs. The silk skirts of her expensive dress rustled around her. The rings she loved to wear hung heavy on her fingers. By her side walked one of the little lap dogs she loved and pampered.

Her servants had gone back to the mansion after assuring her that the cliffs were empty of beggars. Agatha strolled along the stone cliffs, worn smooth by years of crashing waves. Ahead of her, a large rock jutted into the path. To pass by it, she had to walk close to the edge of the cliff. Her tiny dog began to whimper and wouldn't go further. Agatha snapped her fingers at him angrily, but the dog cowered on the ground. Finally, she bent down and picked him up, and then stepped cautiously around the rock onto the narrow path.

Below, the sea was surging and foaming with the tide. The water looked dark and angry with the sunlight fading in the sky. Agatha had almost walked around the rock when she looked up from the ocean and saw an old woman sitting on a ledge in the rock. With a scream Agatha dropped her little dog. It scampered to safety away from the cliff edge.

"Some food for the starving," the old woman begged in a cracked voice.

Agatha looked at the beggar with disgust. The woman was dressed in black rags with an old black cape thrown around her shoulders. Her yellowed teeth were long and pointed. Her dark eyes seemed to glow in her old, wrinkled face. And her gnarled fingers shook as they reached out to Agatha, pleading.

"Go away, old woman," Agatha said. She wanted to run away herself, but her legs had become weak with fright.

"Rich lady, I am starving," the old woman said. "Give me just one coin to buy food with."

"Leave me alone," Agatha screamed. But still she couldn't run away from the woman. Their eyes met, and Agatha felt fear creep through her veins like a bitter poison.

"If you do not give me something to eat, I will die," the old beggar woman said in a shaking voice. "And someday, you will be like me, poor and ugly and starving."

Agatha twisted her eyes away from the woman's gaze. "I'll never be like you," she hissed. Then she looked down at the rings on her hands and pulled from one finger a gold ring engraved with her initials.

"I can never be poor," she said, "just as this ring can never return from the sea." Then she threw the ring over the cliff into the roaring ocean.

The old woman muttered strange words and looked out to the sea. Agatha suddenly found her strength and ran back along the cliff path to her mansion.

That night Agatha did not enjoy the delicious meal set before her on the long table. The roast beef tasted dry in her mouth, even though it had been cooked to perfection. The rich chocolate dessert seemed bitter rather than sweet, and Agatha pushed it away uneaten. She walked to the fireplace and sat down in a chair in front of it. But when she stared into the flames, she seemed to see the old woman's eyes glowing back at her.

The next evening she began to take her walk on the cliffs again. But a servant hurried to stop her. He said he had found a dead body on a rock ledge and had called the villagers to take it away. Mrs. Parry would have to wait until the woman was removed.

Agatha hurried back into her mansion. She didn't have to ask what the woman looked like. She knew exactly how the old, wrinkled face would look in death.

That night was Agatha's first of many sleepless nights. She put on her lace and silk nightgown, lay her head down on the goose-feather pillows, shut her eyes, and saw the old woman's glowing eyes, yellow teeth, and gnarled fingers.

A year passed. Agatha's once plump figure had become thin and bony, and her rich clothes hung loose on her. She no longer took walks along the cliffs, and her complexion had grown dry and wrinkled. Doctors were called to help her sleep and eat, but they did no good.

Agatha became greedier and greedier as she became thinner and thinner. During the nights when she couldn't sleep, she counted her money or rearranged her jewels in her drawers. Often she thought of the gold ring she had thrown into the sea.

One night she decided she would have a grand dinner and invite all her rich friends whom she hadn't seen for over a year. She must let them know that she was still rich and well, just in case they had heard rumors to the opposite. She sent her servants to buy the most expensive foods and wines for the dinner. She ordered delicacies from all over the world. No expense was spared to get the mansion ready.

At last the night of the great dinner arrived. Agatha's old friends poured into the house, curious and eager to see her. She noticed the surprise on their faces when she greeted them. With artificial smiles, they told her how well she looked.

Agatha led them into the dining room, where the long table was set with sparkling silver and shining china. She took her place at the head of the table and gestured to the servants to begin serving. The guests ate their first, second, and third courses while Agatha watched. She left the food put on her plate untouched, for she had no appetite.

Then a servant came in carrying a large,

domed platter. He set it on the table in front of Agatha and, with a flourish, whisked off the top. Under the dome was a huge whole fish. The guests let out a murmur of amazement.

The servant picked up a knife and began to carve the fish. He cut down its long body and then opened it up. Suddenly, with a loud clatter, he dropped the knife on the silver plate. Agatha looked up at the servant with irritation, then she followed his eyes down to the platter.

There, inside the fish's belly, was a gold ring, shining in the candlelight. The servant picked it up and handed it to Agatha. With trembling fingers, she turned it around and around until she saw her initials etched in the gold. She remembered the words she had spoken when she threw the ring in the sea. Then, as her guests watched with curious eyes, Agatha jumped up and ran from the table, choking back the scream that was rising in her throat.

That night a fire burned Agatha's house to the ground, destroying all her riches. Agatha escaped with just the clothes she had on and a tattered black cape that a servant had put around her. At daybreak, Agatha stood watching the last embers of her house burn out. Then she pulled the cape closer around her and walked toward the cliffs overlooking the ocean.

And to this day, if you go to a certain place along the cliffs of New England, you might see the ghost of an old beggar woman. And you'll know who she is by the tattered black cape and the gold ring that she still wears.

The Masked Ball

It was Halloween night. A full moon shone down on the mansion where a large party of people danced and laughed at the masked ball. But upstairs in the mansion, one person was not dancing or laughing.

A young woman named Kate was standing alone in a small room. Holding her silvery mask in shaking hands, she stared at her face in a large gilt-framed mirror. Signs of fear and sleeplessness marked her blue eyes. Quickly she slipped the mask back over her face and turned to the door. She would have to go back to the ball . . . even though, somewhere in the crowd, the vampire waited for her.

Out in the corridor, Kate passed a man in a Roman toga and a woman dressed as Cleopatra. Like Kate, they wore masks over their faces. But even without their masks, Kate wouldn't have known them. She only knew the host of the party, an old acquaintance of her father's.

Kate came to the top of the wide, spiral staircase that wound down to the front hallway of the mansion. From below, the sound of laughing and talking floated up to her. Kate put on an artificial smile and, step by step, started down the staircase.

Halfway down, her eyes were caught by a dark figure gliding through the crowd. His black cape swirled as he moved through the brightly colored costumes. Kate's heart skipped a beat, and her knees turned to sand. It was the same man she had glimpsed earlier and run away from. She had only seen his black clothes and his dark, shiny hair. But she knew who he was — the vampire.

Kate forced herself to take another step down the stairs. Then the man turned around and looked up, staring straight at her. In one terrible second, Kate saw the two fangs curving over his red lips. She felt the strength in her legs ebb away. Then her mind went black. . . .

When she opened her eyes, the blackness had gone. Kate looked up into the masked face of a young man with blond hair.

"Are you all right?" he asked.

Kate stood up straight on the staircase and remembered where she was. Many of the masked faces in the hallway below were turned toward her. But the dark figure with the horrible fangs was nowhere to be seen.

"Let me help you down the stairs," the young man said.

Kate turned to him and smiled. He was dressed in a red braided jacket and black pants. A full mask covered his face.

"Thank you," she said. "I must have started to faint."

"Come with me," the young man said. "Perhaps you need something to eat. My name, by the way, is Robert."

"I'm Kate," she answered, feeling as though a shadow had been lifted from the evening.

She walked beside the young man through the crowd of curious masks staring at her. They made their way to the ballroom, where a large table was filled with food. Kate tried to eat a small sandwich but found that her appetite had disappeared.

"I made a fool of myself on the staircase," she said, turning to Robert. "You see, I thought I saw a vampire." She paused and then said, "For many nights now, I have had terrible dreams — nightmares — about a vampire."

Robert stopped eating and stared at her intently. "What are your dreams like?" he asked.

Kate hesitated. She didn't know how her strange story would sound to him. But he waited for her to begin.

"I dream that a vampire dressed all in black is coming to get me," she said. "No matter how I try to escape him, he is always there. And just as I see his fangs, I scream . . . and wake up."

As Kate finished her story, she noticed a change in Robert's eyes. They became harder and darker. Suddenly, she was embarrassed. Perhaps he thought she was crazy.

"I'm sorry," she said. "I'm spoiling your evening. Could we dance?"

Robert took her hand and led her to the dance floor. Soon Kate forgot about the man in black and her nightmare. Then, as another dance began, Kate saw a white hand reach up to Robert's shoulder and tap it. They both turned to face the dark figure standing beside them.

"May I cut in and have this dance with the young lady?" he asked.

Kate shrank back in terror. It was the man in black — the vampire — standing only inches away from her. Her eyes were drawn to his mouth. Now she could see that the fangs were made of plastic and not real at all. But she turned away quickly and gripped Robert's hand tightly in hers.

"I'm sorry," Robert said firmly, "but she wants to stay with me."

Kate watched the black figure slip away like a cat through the crowd.

"That was him, the man I saw before," Kate said as they began to dance again. "Did you see his fangs?"

"They weren't real fangs at all," Robert said. "You shouldn't be afraid of him."

"But I am afraid," Kate said. "My dreams are so real that I'm afraid they might come true."

You are overexcited," Robert said. "It is Halloween night."

His voice sounded hard and cold to Kate, so cold that a chill ran down her spine. Perhaps he was becoming bored by her talk of the vampire. Suddenly Kate wanted to leave the ballroom and breathe fresh air.

"Please come out onto the patio with me," she said. "I can't stand it in here anymore."

Robert led her from the dance floor to a set of French doors that opened up onto the patio. They walked into the warm night air. Kate looked up at the moon in the sky. It still shone brightly, but the shadow of a cloud bank loomed near it.

"Now I feel safe," she said, turning around to look back at the windows of the ballroom. Then she saw the silhouette against the window. It was the vampire, staring out at her on the patio.

Kate choked back a scream and ran down a flight of steps into the garden, pulling Robert along with her.

"It's hard to see," she gasped as they followed a path that twisted among high bushes. "I have to take off my mask." She pulled the silvery mask away from her face and looked at Robert, expecting him to take off his mask as well. But he just stared at her and then hurried down the path.

Suddenly the path ended at the edge of a lake. Kate found herself standing on a narrow wooden dock that had a rowboat tied to it. Robert gestured toward the boat.

"I'll take you for a ride in the moonlight," he said.

Kate stepped into the rowboat. Then, before he got in, Robert unbuttoned his red braid jacket and pulled it off. Kate noticed that now he was dressed all in black. He stepped into the boat, picked up the oars, and pulled the boat away from the dock.

Kate sat up straight in the boat and nervously looked back at the distant lights of the mansion. In front of her, Robert lifted the heavy oars in and out of the water.

"This is hard work," he said. "Would you hold the oars while I take off my wig?"

Kate grasped the oars with both hands and watched with curiosity as he pulled off the blond wig, holding his mask carefully in place with his other hand. As he took the oars back,

Kate noticed how the moonlight shimmered on his shiny black hair.

"Why don't you take off your mask?" Kate asked. "It must be very uncomfortable."

Robert didn't answer, but kept rowing farther and farther away from the shore.

Kate looked up at the moon. It was still shining bright and full, but she could see the corner of the cloud bank drawing nearer to it in the sky. She turned back to look at Robert. His mask looked eerie in the moonlight against the darkness of his hair and clothing.

"Please, take off that mask," Kate asked him.

"When we get to the middle of the lake," he answered. "It will only be a few more minutes."

Kate realized that her heart had begun to pound. She looked wildly around the dark lake, searching for the shoreline. Just then, the clouds passed over the moon. She could only see the shadowy figure in front of her.

Suddenly the sound of the oars lapping in the water stopped. Kate heard them being dragged into the boat. Then all was quiet.

Kate sat very still in the boat as the cold fingers of fear reached around her heart. In the pale light, she could see Robert's hand moving

up to take off the mask. Then the moon broke
out of the clouds, and a scream rose from deep
in Kate's throat.

The light of the moon shone down on the face
of the vampire . . . and glittered on his long
white fangs.

Skin-and-Bones

It was one hundred years ago, on an autumn night, that Jacob Cooper drew his horse and buggy up to the old inn at twilight. As Jacob tied his horse to the hitching post by the side of the inn, he turned back to look at the western sky. It was purplish red from the setting sun and splotched with angry black clouds. A sharp wind had sprung up and was cutting through Jacob's coat and chilling him to the bone.

Jacob hurried toward the door with a sign hanging over it that read: The Red Fox Inn. As he pushed the door open, he felt a rush of warm air and the smell of cooked food. Jacob walked in, meeting the stares of the three men who sat at a table eating and drinking. A red-cheeked man stood behind the bar, polishing its shiny mahogany surface.

"Evening," Jacob said, sitting down at a table. "I'd like some hot roast beef and whatever you have to go with it," he said to the man behind the bar.

"You look half frozen," the man said in a friendly way as he turned to go into the kitchen to get Jacob's food.

"Cold out there?" one of the men at the table said.

Jacob nodded his head and rubbed his hands together.

"Good thing you're at a warm, safe inn," another man said. "I wouldn't want to travel hereabouts on such a night."

"I just stopped for food," Jacob explained as the rosy-cheeked man brought out his food from the kitchen. "I have to travel ten miles yet tonight. My friend in Platkill is expecting me."

Jacob noticed that the four men had fallen silent and were looking at each other uneasily.

"You'd better tell him, Joe," one of the men at the table said to the rosy-cheeked man.

Joe leaned on the bar, cleared his throat, and looked at Jacob.

"Listen, young man, you'd be a fool to travel on to Platkill on a night like this. It's a stretch of empty country with nothing but jagged boulders and thick woods on both sides of the road."

"My horses are good," Jacob said, "and my buggy is in good repair." He stopped and laughed. "And I'm not afraid of driving through a thick woods at night. My friend is expecting me tonight. He'd be worried if I didn't arrive."

There was another stretch of silence as Jacob ate more of his food.

"Go on, Joe, tell him," one of the men urged.

"Now listen to me, young man," Joe began again. "This is strange country around here. It's wild and untamed — not like where I suspect you come from."

"City life can be wild, too," Jacob said with a smile.

"Tell him about Skin-and-Bones, Joe," one of the men said.

"It's not the rocks and the trees I'm trying to warn you about," Joe went on. "It's a creature we call Skin-and-Bones. On nights like this, she likes to trick travelers into giving her a ride. And then they're found the next morning, dead."

Jacob looked from one serious face to another

in the room. Then he burst out laughing.

"You take me for a fool," he said. "I'm not going to be scared by any ghost story."

"But Skin-and-Bones isn't a ghost," Joe said in a deadly serious voice. "She's just skin and bones — almost a skeleton. And when she gets her sharp, bony hands around your neck. . . ."

Jacob threw down his napkin and pushed back his chair. "I've finished my meal, and now I'll be off. Your story was good entertainment. I'll keep it in mind on my journey."

Joe shrugged and took the money Jacob paid him for the meal. Then, as Jacob walked out the door, he called after him, "Good luck. And don't go picking up anybody asking you for a ride."

The cold wind hit Jacob with a blast as he hurried to his buggy. He unhitched the horses and climbed up on the seat. He pulled up the hood as high as it would go to give him shelter from the icy air. Then he slapped the reins against the horses' backs and set off down the road to Platkill.

The last light had faded from the sky, but a full moon lit the road as it snaked through the hills and woods of the rugged landscape. Jacob hummed a song to himself to help keep his spirits up. The cold air was beginning to numb his skin, and his arms were growing tired of holding the horses' reins. And for all his bragging at the inn, he didn't like being out on this deserted road alone at night.

The woods around him were a dense mixture of shadowy fir trees and giant oaks whose bare branches had been stripped of leaves by the wind. Every so often, the buggy would pass an outcropping of rock that gleamed white and ghostly in the moonlight.

Jacob's mind was drifting to thoughts of his friend's warm fireside when, suddenly, his horses let out a strange nickering sound. He looked around him in alarm, and then saw what had upset the horses. A figure was standing by the roadside ahead of him. She had a dark shawl over her head and was reaching out a white arm toward him. The moon was shining on her face, and Jacob could see that it was an old woman beckoning to him.

The story that the men at the inn had told him raced through his mind. His buggy came closer and closer to the woman, but he didn't pull in the reins on his horses. As he passed her by, he saw the look of disappointment on her tired, old face. Jacob thought about turning back to give the woman help, but something inside him whispered that he should go on.

Jacob slapped the reins angrily against the horses' backs and made them race down the road. He felt like a fool. But soon he would reach Platkill and be able to forget all about his journey.

The horses trotted down the lonely road while Jacob shivered on the buggy seat. Then he felt a tension in the reins. The two horses reared back and pranced around on the road, nervous and skittish. It took all Jacob's strength to get them back under control. When they were calm again, he sat on the buggy seat, his heart beating fast, and caught his breath.

Then he saw the slight figure standing by the side of the road. In the moonlight, he could see that she was a young woman with long, reddish-gold hair. She was clutching her green cape around her and looking at him with imploring eyes.

"Sir," she called out. "I need a ride to Platkill. I was thrown off my horse over two hours ago, and I am cold and tired. You're the first person who has come along to help. Could I please have a ride in your carriage?"

Jacob watched the young woman's face as she walked closer. He had seldom seen a woman so lovely, and her voice was soft and refined.

"It would be my pleasure to take you to Platkill," he said, stretching out a hand to help her up onto the buggy seat. "I'm headed there myself tonight, to visit an old friend."

"You're very kind," the young woman said. "I would have frozen in another hour on a night like this."

Jacob pulled his eyes away from her beautiful face that was so close to his now. He slapped the reins on the horses' backs, and the carriage rolled off down the road again.

At first Jacob asked the young woman questions. But she seemed shy and reserved. He realized that she might be frightened of him, a stranger who had picked her up on a lonely road.

For a long while, they traveled on in silence. Every so often, Jacob would glance over at her face. Several times she smiled back at him, her eyes glowing in the moonlight. But then he noticed that her face had set into a hardened expression that didn't change when their eyes met. And even later, when he looked at her,

Jacob thought that she did not look as beautiful as she had at first.

Jacob turned his eyes onto the narrow, dark road in front of him and smiled. Perhaps he had just imagined that she was so beautiful, standing alone on the deserted road in the moonlight. He glanced over at her once more and felt a shock go through his body.

The woman's face no longer looked young. Her skin had lines in it, and her hair looked dull and gray, not reddish gold, in the moonlight. Jacob put the reins in one hand and rubbed his eyes with the other hand. He suddenly felt confused and exhausted. He glanced over to see the woman watching him closely. Her dark eyes seemed to be sunken in their sockets, and her cheekbones stuck out of her thin face.

Jacob shuddered and turned his eyes back to the road. Something was nagging at the back of his mind and making him frightened and nervous. He clenched his teeth and fixed his eyes on the road ahead. According to his calculations, he should be in Platkill in less than fifteen minutes. He would be glad to reach his friend's house and be out of this strange country.

In a flash a prickling feeling started at the back of his neck. It traveled down his spine and then spread through all his body. He willed his eyes to stay on the road, but he could stand it no longer. He turned to look at the woman.

A skeleton sat on the carriage seat beside him, grinning a horrible smile. Jacob knew it was Skin-and-Bones. He gripped the reins in terror and then saw the skeleton's bony hands move out from under her cape and reach for his neck.

Jacob twisted away as Skin-and-Bones's arms lunged for him and clawed at his clothing. He let the reins drop and put his arms up to protect his neck. The bony arms were clutching at him now, and he could barely struggle against their deathly grip. The horses pranced and gallopped wildly down the road.

Jacob felt the sharp, bony fingers closing around his neck. He felt his breath coming in short, desperate gasps. Skin-and-Bones had her face pressed up against his. Jacob pulled together all the life he had left in his body. With a burst of strength he tore away the hands from his neck. Skin-and-Bones reeled back, still grinning her horrible smile. Once again, she lunged for his throat, but Jacob caught her bony wrists in his hands. He wrenched her out of her seat and threw her over the side of the buggy. With a bloodcurdling scream, Skin-and-Bones fell onto the road.

Jacob slumped back in the buggy, half conscious, and let the horses run down the road to Platkill.

"Jacob Cooper, is that you?" a voice was saying.

Jacob opened his eyes to see his friend looking at him with worried eyes.

"Jacob, what's the matter?" his friend asked. "The horses brought you here, but you were unconscious. Are you sick?"

"Skin-and-Bones," Jacob mumbled.

"What nonsense are you talking?" his friend exclaimed.

"Skin-and-Bones," Jacob repeated. "She tried to kill me."

"Did you hear that superstitious old story?" his friend asked, pulling him to the ground. "The local people tell that to frighten travelers."

Jacob rubbed his eyes and looked up at the moonlight. Had it all just been a dream? Then he looked at his friend and saw the expression of horror on his face. Jacob followed his friend's eyes to the side of the buggy.

There, dangling from the hook that had caught it as she fell, was the white, bony hand . . . of Skin-and-Bones.

The Snake Charmer

Lucy Morris sat on the veranda of her parents' house outside the village of Kampur. Servants came and went, adding ice to her lemonade or fetching her a book or treat. Still, Lucy's mouth was set in a pout. She didn't like this foreign place. Her father had come here to do research for three years, but only one month had passed, and to Lucy, it had seemed like an eternity.

The heavy, humid heat made Lucy feel faint. The strong, spicy smells of the food made her lose her appetite. And the insects that scurried about the house made her scream in terror.

Lucy sat on the veranda pouring out all her anger into a letter she was writing her friend back home. Slowly, as she wrote, she became aware of a sound she hadn't heard before. It was a tune, a low, whining tune being played on a flute of some kind. Lucy didn't know how long the music had been playing, but once she was aware of it, she could hear nothing else.

She threw down her pen and paper and got up from the big wicker chair where she had been sitting. Then she walked to the end of the veranda that was near the road. The house sat on a dusty, seldom-traveled road that led to the nearby village. Lucy peered down over the veranda railing and caught her breath at what she saw.

On the ground was an old man, dressed in rags, moving back and forth as he played the flute that was making the hypnotic music she heard. The song repeated itself over and over again in high, whining notes. Lucy was about to call to the man to go away when she noticed the basket sitting in front of him. From a hole in its top, a sinister, flat-headed snake was swaying back and forth to the music.

Lucy screamed when she saw the snake. She had a deathly fear of snakes. The man glanced up at her with his dark eyes and then went on playing the song for his cobra.

Lucy ran back into the house and demanded that the servants tell the man to leave at once.

But the servants shook their heads and muttered that it would bring bad luck to them. Lucy wished her mother and father were at home, but they were gone for three days on a research trip. So Lucy ran back out to the end of the veranda and shouted to the old man to go away.

For a moment, he seemed not to hear her. But Lucy kept shouting and motioning to him. Then suddenly he stopped moving and playing the flute and stared at her with his bottomless, black eyes. The cobra suddenly stopped swaying and turned to look at Lucy, too. The snake's evil-looking eyes seemed to be memorizing her face. Lucy shrank back in fear and ran into the house. Once again, the insidious music began.

The music kept up through dinner and into the evening. When Lucy went to bed, she could still hear the song of the snake charmer's flute. In her mind, she could see the cobra swaying back and forth to the music. After hours of tossing and turning in the hot air, she finally fell asleep.

When Lucy woke up, she noticed a change in the air. It was silent. The music had stopped. Lucy ran to her window that looked out onto the road. Looking back up at her from the ground was the snake charmer. When he saw her face he took up his flute and began to play. The music wound its way through the window into Lucy's brain.

At breakfast she threw a temper tantrum and demanded that the servants get rid of the snake charmer. But once again, they refused. They tried to tell her that such a man had strange powers, but she wouldn't listen. She went to the back of the house as far away from the music as she could get.

Lucy stayed inside the house all morning and all afternoon. But still she could not escape the snake charmer's song. Before dinner, she walked out onto the veranda and called to the man.

"I will give you money," she said, "if you'll just go away. What is it you want?"

The man played his song for several more minutes. Then he stopped and looked up at her.

"Something that belongs to you," he said, showing chipped, yellowed teeth. "A lock of your golden hair."

Just then, the cobra reared its head toward Lucy. She shrank back and ran into the house, shutting the door tightly behind her. But the music started up again, like a mad tune in her brain.

Lucy spent another restless night, tossing and turning, and covering her head with a pillow to keep out the sound of the music. She woke so late the next morning that the snake charmer had already started playing by the time she got up. Lucy wasn't sure she could stand it any longer.

She sat down in front of her mirror and started to brush her long, blonde hair. Then she remembered the snake charmer's wish. She picked up a lock of her hair and thought how she would hate to cut it. But if that would get rid of the man and his horrible music, perhaps it would be worth losing.

Lucy searched her drawers for a pair of scissors. She couldn't find one anywhere. She opened her closet doors to see if any were among her childhood toys stored there. At last she found a pair in a box with colored paper and crayons. Then something else caught her eye in the stack of toys in the closet. It was a doll she'd been given when she was six, a doll with long, blonde hair. Her mother had told her the hair was real.

Lucy pulled the doll from her closet and held its head up to hers in front of the mirror. Their hair colors matched perfectly. Lucy laid the doll down on her bed and snipped off a lock of its hair and rushed from the room.

Lucy ran out to the end of the veranda and called to the snake charmer. He kept playing his song until she held up the lock of golden hair for him to see. Then he put down his flute and reached up to take the hair.

Lucy saw the strange look on his face as he took the hair from her hands. She saw the cobra's evil eyes staring at her again. Then the snake showed its short fangs at her.

"Now go away!" she screamed and ran back into the house.

All that morning and afternoon, the house was perfectly still. Just before dinner, a friend of her mother's came to visit Lucy. She said that Lucy's parents would be returning from their trip that night. Lucy felt the happiest she had been since coming to Kampur. She was rid of the snake charmer and his music. And soon her parents would be home.

They came later than she expected, long after dinner was over and when it was almost time for Lucy to go to bed. Lucy hugged her mother and father and then waited for the presents she knew they'd bring. Right after she opened the presents, she began to tell the story of the snake charmer and his endless music.

"But how did you get him to leave?" her mother asked.

"He wanted a lock of my hair," Lucy said. "So I gave him a lock of hair."

"No, Lucy," her father gasped. "You didn't do that! Not to a man like that!"

"Yes, I did," Lucy said. "I gave him a lock of hair. . . ."

She didn't have a chance to finish. Her father jumped to his feet and ran toward her bedroom. Lucy ran after him, trying to tell the rest of her story. But Mr. Morris didn't stop until he reached her bedroom door and threw it open. Lucy ran up beside him as he turned on the lights. Together they stared in horror at the thing on the bed.

Lucy's blonde-haired doll still lay there. And wrapped around it in a death grip . . . was the evil-eyed cobra of the snake charmer.

The Snipe Hunt

The twelve boys sat around the campfire, roasting marshmallows on sticks after finishing their evening meal. Their faces were lit by the jumping flames of the fire — eight older faces and four younger faces. The older boys looked relaxed and confident. But the younger boys looked tense and worried. Tonight they would be tested.

Ty, who was only eleven, was the youngest boy in the group. Jimmy, Paul, and Brad were twelve, but this was their initiation night, too. If they made it through tonight, they'd be let into the camping club.

"What do you think they'll do to us?" Ty whispered to Brad, who sat beside him by the fire.

"I don't know," Brad answered. "Ask Paul. His brother is one of the older guys."

Ty turned to Paul on his other side. "What will they do to us tonight?" he asked in a low voice.

"I heard my brother talk about a snipe hunt," Paul whispered back.

"A snipe hunt?" Ty said. "What's that?"

Before Paul could answer, Mark, one of the leaders, started to talk. Everyone paid attention.

"I want to warn you younger guys about something," Paul began. "These woods are pretty far from civilization. We're out here in the middle of nowhere by ourselves, and we have to be careful. Nobody knows for sure what kind of animals are in the woods — wolves, bears, bobcats. We've had our supper . . . but they might still be hungry."

Ty looked at Brad nervously. Brad's face had grown serious, too.

"And there's another thing I have to tell you," Mark went on. "I heard something on the radio today, just before we left to come here. I've been trying to decide whether or not to tell you, but now I think I should. A murderer escaped from the state penitentiary in Columbus last night. The police haven't caught him yet, but they know he headed in a northwest direction. They figure he's covering about twenty miles a day . . . and, well, you know about where that would take him."

"This place is about twenty miles northwest of Columbus," Brad said.

"Yeah, that's right," Mark said. "But now that we're here, I don't think we should call off our camping trip just because of an escaped murderer."

Ty noticed that his hands were shaking so much that his marshmallow stick was moving up and down. The marshmallow had burned to a crisp.

"So be careful, and report anything strange that you hear or see in the woods," Mark said.

Just then, there was a loud crack in the woods behind the younger boys. They all jumped and turned around.

"What was that?" Ty whimpered.

The older boys laughed.

"What's the matter, Ty, getting a little scared?" Robbie asked.

"It's too early to get scared," Mark said.

"You four guys have to go on your snipe hunt yet. Go to your tents and get a flashlight and get back here in five minutes."

The boys got up from the campfire and walked back to their tents through the chilly night air. The moon was full enough to light their way, but the dark shadows of the trees made it hard to see far into the dense woods. They all got their flashlights from their packs and started back to the campfire.

"Was he telling the truth about the murderer?" Ty whispered to Paul on the way back.

"I don't know," Paul said. "And I don't want to find out."

"I wish this were over with!" Jimmy said.

Mark was waiting for them. He was standing by the fire with four burlap bags.

"These are the bags you use to catch the snipe," he said, handing one to each of the boys.

"How do we know it's a snipe?" Jimmy asked. "What's it look like?"

"Listen, you'll know when you see it," Mark said. "Now be quiet and listen to the rules."

The four boys clutched their bags in one hand and their flashlights in the other and listened.

"Each of you has to walk in a different direction from the campfire," Mark began.

"Count how many steps you're taking, and when you get to two hundred fifty, stop. That'll take you far enough away from the light of the campfire. Snipes are too smart to come near a fire."

"What about our flashlights?" Ty asked. "Won't they scare away the snipes?"

Some of the older boys started to laugh. But Mark cut them off.

"Use your flashlights while you're walking out the two hundred fifty steps. Then turn them off and wait."

"How long do we wait?" Brad asked.

"Till we call you in with this whistle," Mark said. He sounded three short whistles and then three long whistles.

"Any questions?"

The four boys looked at each other uneasily.

"What about those other animals you talked about?" Paul said. "What if we see them?"

"Or the murderer?" Ty added with a whisper.

Mark just shrugged his shoulders and looked at his watch.

"Time to start walking," he said. "And remember to count two hundred fifty steps. Then turn off your lights."

Ty glanced over at Paul and Brad and Jimmy. They looked as scared as he felt. Mark told Brad to start walking toward the north. Then he sent Jimmy off to the east and Paul to the west.

"Ty," he said, "you walk south."

Ty gulped, switched on his flashlight, and turned to face the south. He took a step away from the campfire and started counting. At first he took long steps; then he took shorter ones that wouldn't carry him so far into the woods.

Ty had counted a hundred steps when he first turned around. The campfire was just a yellowish glow in the darkness of the woods. He shone his light into the woods in front of him and started walking and counting again. The dead leaves that had fallen from the trees crackled under his feet. Several times a raised root caught at his foot and almost sent him sprawling onto the ground. Night animals scurried away as his light pierced the darkness. Once an owl swooped down across the moon and passed its shadow over him.

Ty had counted two hundred steps. He turned around. The thick trees blocked out the campfire now. He couldn't hear the older boys' voices and laughter anymore. He hoped he would be able to hear Mark's whistles.

Fifty more steps to go. Ty forced his legs to go on through the woods until he had counted to two hundred fifty. Then he swung his flashlight around in the place where he had stopped. It was a small clearing that had a thick carpet of leaves covering the ground.

The flashlight picked up the outline of a big tree stump about three yards from where Ty stood. Tall hickory trees with shaggy bark stood around the small clearing. Ty pointed the light up and saw their long limbs reaching up to the sky like the arms of skeletons. Then he flicked off the flashlight and crouched down on the ground. He clutched the burlap bag in both hands and waited. The snipe hunt had begun.

The wind blew through the tree branches above him, making a strange rattling sound. Ty waited and waited. Once he saw a big shadow move near the tree stump. He froze, not sure if it was a bear or a man. But the shadow disappeared and didn't come back again. Ty's hands were growing numb with cold and fatigue. He thought he would go crazy if he had to stay out in the dark alone one more minute.

Then he heard a strange noise come from the

direction of the tree stump. It was a shrill animal sound, unlike anything he'd ever heard before. He strained his eyes to see in the moonlight. He glimpsed the pale, gray body of an animal walking toward him from the tree stump. It kept making its shrill call as it slowly wobbled across the bed of leaves.

Ty had never seen an animal like it before. He knew it must be a snipe. He leaned over and set the burlap bag down in front of where the animal was walking. It didn't seem to be able to see the bag and headed straight toward it. Ty held his breath until the small animal had walked into his bag. Then he shut the opening of the bag and gripped it tight.

A minute later, three short whistles and three long whistles cut through the stillness of the night. Ty picked up his flashlight and started to run in the direction of the sound. He held the sack away from his body and listened as the animal begin to make shrill noises in a panic.

Ty burst into the light of the campfire with his breath coming in short gasps. Everyone else was standing there, waiting for him. Paul, Brad, and Jimmy had already made it back.

"We thought the murderer might have got you, Ty," Mark said. The boys around the campfire laughed. Ty stood by the fire with his bag, waiting for Mark to ask about the snipe. But Mark didn't even look at his bag.

"The four of you did a great job," he said, looking at Paul, Brad, Jimmy, and Ty. "None of you chickened out. You all passed the test, and now you're in the club."

"But what about the snipe?" Ty asked.

"Come on, Ty, that was just a joke," Robbie said.

"Ty, what do you have in that bag?" Mark asked.

"A snipe," Ty answered.

Just then, the animal cried its weird call.

"He caught something!" Brad said. "Let's see it."

Everyone jumped up and crowded around Ty.

"Drop the bag into this box, Ty," Mark ordered, pulling over an empty food box.

Carefully Ty put the bag into the box and let go of its opening. The other boys peered down into the box. Slowly, the animal Ty had caught crawled out of the bag. It turned its face up at the boys staring down at it. Then it let out a hiss and a shrill screech.

The boys all jumped back.

"What is it?" Robbie asked.

"That's the strangest-looking animal I've ever seen," Mark said.

Again the boys stared down at the animal. It had short gray fur and a thick, stout body. Its paws had sharp white claws and its long tail ended in a jagged point. But its head was weirdest of all. The ears were high and pointed, and the mouth had four long, sharp teeth.

"I think it's a baby that was just born," Mark said. "Its eyes are still shut."

"Look, it's trying to open them," Ty said.

Suddenly the animal's strange eyes flew open. They were orange and glowed in the night.

"Is it a snipe?" Ty asked.

"I don't know," Mark said. "Nobody's ever seen a snipe. We just made up the snipe hunt to scare you guys."

"So what is it?" Brad asked.

The animal started to shriek louder and louder and show its pointed teeth at the boys.

One by one, they backed uneasily away from the box.

"What was that?" Robbie suddenly asked, turning around to look into the woods. "I thought I heard something out there."

"Me, too," said Paul.

The boys fell silent and listened as the animal in the box made its shrill call over and over again. And from different parts of the woods, the same call came back.

"What are we going to do?" Ty asked.

"I don't know," Mark answered, looking scared.

The calls from the woods became louder and louder. Then the leaves on the floor of the woods started to rustle. The boys huddled closer together around the campfire.

Suddenly Ty screamed and pointed to the woods. A pair of strange orange eyes were glowing from the shadows of the trees. They were like the eyes of the animal in the box, only bigger. Then Brad screamed and pointed to the opposite side of the campfire. The boys whirled around and saw another pair of orange eyes glowing in the woods. Then they saw another and another and another.

The animal in the box made a weird noise from deep in its throat. Then from the woods, like a nightmarish echo, came the same noise from all around the boys.

Mark looked at Ty's face, which had turned white with fear.

"You caught a snipe, all right," he said.

Then they turned to look at the orange eyes in the woods. The eyes had started to glow brighter. And they were moving in closer and closer . . . toward the twelve boys huddled together around the campfire.